Chapter One
ARCTIC ALERT

Kiki put down the wrench and wiped her forehead. It was hot in the school yard, and the Ghanaian sun was beating down on her shoulders. She had almost fixed her friend's bike, but the gears still weren't moving smoothly.

"Is it working now?" asked her friend, Abina.

THE SECRET EXPLORERS ®
AND THE MISSING SCIENTIST

CONTENTS

"It just needs a little oil," Kiki explained.

She turned to her tools, laid out neatly on the upturned box beside her. Taking up the small can of oil, she angled the spout into the bike chain and squirted a few drops among the cogs. Then she turned the pedals and listened to the gentle clicking of the chain.

"It should work better now," she said.

"They're not squeaking at all," exclaimed Abina. "You are an engineering queen, Kiki."

Kiki felt a rush of pride. Working on machinery was her favourite thing. She planned to be an engineer when she was older, fixing things and making people smile the way that Abina was smiling at her now.

She waved as Abina cycled away down the dusty road towards her house. As she tucked her wrench and screwdriver into the special side pocket on her school bag, a glow of light caught her eye. She looked up.

Shining on the pale blue schoolroom door was a symbol that Kiki knew well. With a cry of delight, she touched the matching badge on her school uniform. The compass sign of the Secret Explorers! The letters N, S, E, and W gleamed around its edges. It meant there was a mission!

Kiki zipped her bag shut and ran up the steps towards the schoolroom door, reaching for the symbol with her hand. As her fingers touched the glowing compass, the door swung open. She walked through, screwing her eyes shut in the blinding white light. A blast of cool wind rippled through her hair.

The light dimmed and the wind quietened. Kiki opened her eyes and grinned at the familiar surroundings of the

Exploration Station, with its black stone walls and computer monitors set around the room. In the centre of the floor was a map of the world, and a shimmering image of the Milky Way was on the domed ceiling. Glass cases displayed the objects that the Secret Explorers had collected on their missions, including fossils, meteorites, and feathers.

Kiki ran her fingers over the computer keyboards on her way towards the comfy sofas at the end of the room. "Kiki, here!" she announced.

"Tamiko – here!" A girl with a Stegosaurus clip in her hair came into the room. Tamiko was the Dinosaur Explorer.

Next to arrive was a tall girl brushing mud from her hands. "Leah, here!" she said. Leah was the Biology Explorer, and full of knowledge about plants and animals.

"Ollie – here!" said a red-haired boy in a green T-shirt with a parrot on it. He was the Rainforest Explorer.

Next was a boy with dark curly hair. "Gustavo – here!" he said with a cheerful wave. Gustavo was from Brazil, and he was the History Explorer of the group.

"Cheng – here!" said a dark-haired boy

with a ready smile. Cheng was the Geology Explorer. His pockets were often full of rocks.

"Roshni – here!" said a girl with her hair tied back in a long plait. As the Space Explorer, Roshni knew all about stars, planets and galaxies.

"Connor – here!" The Marine Explorer of the group wore waders, and dripped water on the floor of the Exploration Station. "Didn't have time to change," Connor said apologetically. "What's the mission?"

"We don't know yet," said Cheng.

"But we're about to find out," Kiki said. "Look!"

They turned to the huge map of the world on the floor. A light was shining on the far north of the map.

"That's the Arctic," said Roshni with interest.

"How do you know?" asked Leah.

"There are lots of space observatories in the Arctic," Roshni said. "There's no light pollution, so you can see the stars more clearly."

An image projected from the map. It showed a big ship with a red hull lying in a bay full of white ice. The sky looked grey and heavy with snow.

Gustavo shivered. "Brr! I feel cold just looking at it."

Kiki studied the ship. It was lying at a strange angle in the ice. Was something wrong?

The badge on her school uniform lit up. "Yes!" she said triumphantly. She was going on the mission! She'd never seen snow before.

Connor's badge lit up too. "Looks like I'm joining you, Kiki," he said, beaming.

"Weird choice," observed Ollie. "You normally get missions out in the middle of the ocean, Connor."

"The Arctic is mostly ice," Connor pointed out. "Hardly any land at all. So I guess it makes sense that they want a Marine Explorer!"

"True," said Leah. "And we all know that the Exploration Station never makes a mistake."

Kiki couldn't wait to get started. She ran towards a big red button in the wall and pushed it. The other Explorers stepped back. The floor shivered and opened. Up rose what looked like a battered old go-kart, with a metal steering wheel and peeling paint on its splintered sides.

"Looking as beautiful as ever, Beagle," commented Cheng cheerfully.

The Secret Explorers all laughed. The Beagle wouldn't look like that for long. It was named after the ship sailed by Charles Darwin, the famous scientist, and had lots of secrets too.

Kiki sprang into the old go-kart and settled her hands on the dented metal steering wheel. "Come on, Connor!" she said eagerly.

Connor was hopping around the room, pulling off his waders. "I'm coming as fast as I can!" he said, throwing the waders aside and scrambling into the go-kart.

"Good luck," said Leah. "Remember to call us if you need any help."

"We will," Kiki promised.

She pressed the "START" button. The Beagle shuddered and shook. A bright white light washed over Kiki and Connor as the old go-kart took off, bumping and rattling. Kiki had to hold on tightly. She felt the old steering wheel transforming under her hands, stretching out into a set of handlebars with two rubber throttles and a set of controls. Her fingers were suddenly covered in thick gloves.

There was a final roar of wind and the rattling, rocking feeling stopped.

Kiki could see her own breath for the first time in her life.

She stared at the snowy landscape. It wasn't pure white, like she had imagined. With the light playing over the snow, she could see blue and grey and green shadows too. The snow stood around them in fantastic shapes, carved by the Arctic wind.

So this is the Arctic! she thought in wonder.

"The Beagle is a snowmobile!" gasped Connor. "How cool is this?"

Kiki admired the sleek shape of the snowmobile, with its chunky padded seat and the go-fast flash down its white sides. It had a glass windshield, a set of skis at the front and a caterpillar-track tread at the back to help it grip the ice. "Pretty cool," she agreed, turning round to look at Connor.

Connor was wearing brightly coloured

snow gear, with padded trousers and a cosy down-filled jacket. Kiki was wearing the same thing. The cold air bit at her nose, but the rest of her was as warm as toast.

"There's our mission right there." Connor pointed with a gloved hand. "That ship!"

Kiki turned to the front again. The red hull of the ship lay some distance away, where the ice met a strip of unfrozen, iron-grey sea on the horizon.

"I bet you know how to drive a snowmobile," Connor asked. "You're great at all the tech."

Kiki laughed. "Well, we don't have them in Ghana, that's for sure! But I know about engines. I'm sure I can figure it out. And I know the Beagle will help."

The Beagle gave an encouraging *BEEP*.

A red button glowed on the handlebars. Kiki pressed it, and heard the snowmobile leap into life. She turned the throttle on the right, feeding fuel to the engine so that it roared. The snowmobile began to move smoothly forwards. The skis at the front carved through the snow, while the tread at the back gripped the ice and stopped the snowmobile from skidding.

Kiki grinned. This was fun! She turned the throttle harder. The engine roared again and the Beagle leaped away, zooming through the snow towards their mission.

Chapter Two
TRAPPED IN THE ICE

As they got nearer to the ship, Kiki could see that it was tilting to one side. It seemed to be stuck against a shelf of ice. Overhead, a flock of gulls screeched and beat their wings, swooping through the Arctic sky. Everything here was enormous: the sky, the rocks, the ice. Kiki had never felt so small.

"The ship doesn't look good," Connor

said behind her.

"Not good at all," Kiki agreed.

They were close now to the red hull of the ship. Kiki put on the Beagle's brakes, sending up a plume of snow which spattered her face. It felt like little needles on her skin.

"Looks like we need to help free the ship from the ice," Connor said.

Kiki nodded thoughtfully.

"What kind of ship do you think it is?" Connor asked.

Kiki stared up at the huge red hull. "There are no nets, like you'd see on a fishing boat," she said with a frown.

"No metal crates either," said Connor. "So it's not a container ship. Hey, look!" He pointed to the white lettering on the ship's side. "That must be its name – *The Explorer*."

"Like us!" said Kiki. "Maybe it's some kind

of research ship?"

The ship had run into an ice shelf that rose several metres above the water. Kiki studied the sloping ice. "Let's ride the Beagle up the ice to the deck," she said. "Then we can go aboard and find out for ourselves."

Starting up the engine again, Kiki steered the Beagle onwards. The dark sea beyond the ice shelf looked forbidding and cold. Kiki tried not to think about what would happen if the Beagle lost its grip and slid into the water. But the skis at the front of the snowmobile glided along, and the caterpillar tread at the back kept the Beagle on track.

At the top of the slope, Kiki turned off the engine and climbed off the snowmobile. There was a large "H" painted on the deck – for helicopters, she guessed.

"Hello!" she called across the empty deck of the ship. "Is anyone there?"

A tall man in dark blue overalls appeared through a metal door. He blinked at Kiki and Connor in surprise.

"We saw your ship," Connor explained.

"And we thought you might need help," added Kiki.

"That's very kind of you!" said the man. "Please come aboard." He scratched his beard. "Forgive my surprise. We don't get many unexpected visitors out here. My name is Dr Andersen. Welcome!"

"What kind of ship is this?" Connor asked curiously.

"*The Explorer* is a research ship," Dr Anderson explained.

Connor grinned at Kiki. She had guessed correctly.

"We're in the Arctic to study the effects of climate change," Dr Andersen continued.

"Sea levels are rising all over the world, aren't they?" said Connor. "It's really bad for marine life."

"That's right," said Dr Andersen. "As the world gets warmer, the ice at the Arctic is melting, and huge chunks are breaking off and floating away. That's what caused the problem here."

He pointed at the ice blocking the ship's way out to sea.

"A huge piece of the ice shelf across the bay fell away. Sea ice crashed into our ship, pinning it against another shelf of ice." He sighed. "We can't break *The Explorer* free."

"Have you radioed for help?" Kiki asked.

Dr Andersen shook his head. "The communications mast was damaged in the collision," he said. "But my colleague, Dr Mikkelsen, has gone on her snowmobile to fetch help from a research centre not too far inland. So don't worry, someone should be coming to our rescue any moment now. Come inside! It's cold out here."

Dr Andersen took Kiki and Connor up a flight of metal stairs to a large room with wide windows looking out over the sea ice.

Kiki gazed at the banks of dials and screens. She'd never seen so much technology all in one place. There were weather balloons to monitor atmospheric conditions, and sonar equipment for tracking pods of whales and mapping the sea floor.

"This is the bridge," Dr Andersen told them. "It's the control centre for the whole ship. Our central mission is collecting ice core samples. Come with me down to the laboratory. I can

show you the results of our most recent survey."

Kiki and Connor followed the scientist down a metal staircase and through several narrow corridors. Through half-open cabin doors, Kiki glimpsed beds and desks for the ship's crew.

Dr Andersen opened the door to a small cluttered room full of equipment. "This is where we examine the ice samples that we take," he said.

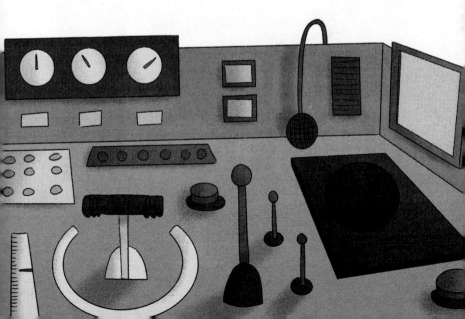

Kiki and Connor gazed at the long cylinders of ice inside the tank in front of them. They shimmered with surprising colours: purple, white, and blue. Kiki glimpsed air bubbles trapped inside.

"We collect samples like this with a special drill," Dr Andersen said. "We drill right down deep where the ice is very old. See those air bubbles? We can study them to find out what the Earth's atmosphere was like thousands of years ago." "Wow!" said Connor. "Time travel in an ice lolly!"

"Exactly," said Dr Andersen. "For example, we know from the air bubbles that there was once less carbon dioxide in the air than there is today. This extra carbon dioxide is contributing to global warming."

Dr Andersen led them back through the ship. He pointed out the engine room, and the 'moon pool': a space set into the hull which allowed the scientists to raise and lower equipment into the water without worrying about rough waves or ice.

Kiki's mind was whirling by the time they returned to the bridge. Connor looked thoughtful too. The crew on the ship were clearly doing amazing work in this incredible, important place.

Dr Andersen checked his watch. "Dr Mikkelsen should have been back with help by now," he said, looking worried. "Perhaps she's lost."

"Does she have a GPS tracker?" Kiki asked. "Can you find her that way?"

"Of course. But with our damaged communications equipment, we can't locate her," said Dr Andersen. He frowned. "If we had another snowmobile, I'd go out there and look for her myself."

Kiki and Connor looked at each other. Suddenly, the way to complete their mission was clear.

"We have a snowmobile, Dr Andersen,"
said Kiki. "We'll go and find Dr Mikkelsen
for you!"

Chapter Three
SNOWY SEARCH

"Have you got the coordinates Dr Andersen gave you, Kiki?" asked Connor.

Kiki adjusted her gloves and put her hands on the handlebars. "I've got coordinates for the research centre and Dr Mikkelsen's tracker data. I've already input everything into our GPS," she said. "We've got to find the doctor first. Ready to go, Beagle?"

The Beagle beeped as Kiki pressed the "START" button and turned the throttle. She manoeuvred the snowmobile around in a half-circle until they were facing down the sloping ice shelf. Then she gunned the engine. The Beagle sped smoothly down the slope and out into the snowy wilderness that lay all around. The wind buffeted her face, but Kiki was warm and cosy in her thick layers of thermal clothing.

Dr Mikkelsen's signal led them east. After a short distance, Kiki saw a set of snowmobile tracks carved into the snow ahead of them. "Those must be her tracks. We should be able to follow them right to her," she said, pointing them out to Connor.

"But what if it's someone else?" Connor asked.

Kiki raised her eyebrows. "Unlikely!" she said with a grin. "I haven't seen a single other person out here."

Connor laughed. "I guess there aren't that many people hanging around the Arctic," he agreed.

They sped on, following Dr Mikkelsen's snowmobile tracks. The light was bright against the snow, even with the grey skies overhead.

Kiki had no idea snow could cover everything so completely. It softened the edges of the land and blurred the horizon, wrapping the world in a huge, fluffy blanket.

The incredible landscape was a lot more varied than she had expected too. There were broken plateaus of ice as well as flat plains, and she had to steer the Beagle around several large, craggy outcroppings. On the horizon lay a range of mountains, which Kiki guessed were parts of frozen islands. The ice looked bluer in some places than others, and she instinctively avoided those. Even though she'd never seen snow, or stepped on ice before, it wasn't hard to work out that in those blue patches, the ice was thinner and less stable.

"Watch out for that crevasse!" Connor called over her shoulder through the biting Arctic wind. He pointed at a great long gash in the ice to the west, where the icy sides were sheer and a deep, dark blue. "We don't want to fall in and end up in the sea underneath!"

The Beagle skimmed across the vast whiteness, carving up the snow ahead of them and leaving caterpillar tracks behind. The tracks from Dr Mikkelsen's snowmobile stretched ahead of them, clear and deep.

"Wow!" said Connor suddenly. "Look at those holes in the ice, Kiki!"

Kiki wiped the snow crystals from her face. "Don't worry," she said. "I'll drive round them!"

"Can you stop the snowmobile?" asked Connor. "I think I know what they are..."

Kiki turned off the engine, which ticked away into silence. Now all they could hear was the wind.

Connor climbed off the snowmobile and made his way across to the ice holes, hunkering down so that he could see into the water.

"These are where seals come up for air," he said.

Connor stiffened suddenly, and beckoned Kiki over.

"Can you see?" he whispered. His eyes were bright with excitement.

The water was almost black, rippling and flowing beneath the ice. At first, Kiki couldn't see anything. Then she glimpsed something moving, far below. Something large, and dappled, swimming strongly through the dark water.

"Ringed seals!" Connor breathed. He crouched closer to the hole. "Loads of them! Ringed seals can swim underwater for forty-five minutes, hunting fish and crustaceans, before they need to come up for air."

Kiki tried to imagine what that was like. "How do they hold their breath for so long?" she wondered.

"They're able to store more oxygen in their bodies than we can," Connor explained. "That keeps them going between breaths." He stood up again and dusted the snow from his knees. "I guess we'd better leave them to it. We don't want to frighten them off. If they see our shadows, they might think that we're polar bears."

Kiki laughed – then stopped. This was the Arctic. *There really are polar bears here*, she thought. And if a polar bear was nearby, they'd never see it. It would be too well camouflaged against the snow...

"Let's get out of here," she suggested, backing a little nervously towards the Beagle. "We've still got to find Dr Mikkelsen."

They set off again. The Beagle's engine sounded extremely loud in all the silence of the snow. Kiki bent over the handlebars and revved the engine as hard as she could. If Dr Mikkelsen was lost, like Dr Andersen feared, then time wasn't on their side. A person could freeze out here in minutes.

Dr Mikkelsen's tracks headed steadily away from them. It wasn't much further to the research station Dr Andersen had mentioned. Perhaps the scientist had made it there after all. Perhaps they would meet a convoy of rescue vehicles coming the other way.

The terrain was more broken here, with jagged cliffs of ice rearing above them. Kiki followed the tracks around a sharp bend. She almost oversteered as the treads at the back of the Beagle swung out wide, throwing up great clods of snow that fell on her shoulders and got into her mouth and nose. She pulled hard, away from the cliff, before the snowmobile could tip over. That was close!

Connor suddenly gasped. Kiki looked around.

An upended snowmobile lay in a heap of snow just beneath the icy cliff. It looked like Dr Mikkelsen had oversteered her snowmobile too – with less successful results.

Kiki slammed on the brakes.

"Dr Mikkelsen!" called Connor. His voice echoed around the icy cliffs. "Hello?"

Kiki scanned the area. Where was she? The snowmobile was clearly wrecked beyond repair. There was no sign of its driver.

"I hope she hasn't been hurt," said Connor anxiously.

Kiki climbed off the Beagle. She knelt down and studied the trampled snow around the wrecked snowmobile. "There's no blood," she said. "So that's good."

"I think she swerved to avoid something," Connor said.

Kiki realised that Connor was right. Unlike their own swerve from taking the bend too fast, the tracks from Dr Mikkelsen's snowmobile were more complicated.

Kiki tracked the wavering tread marks. It looked as if the scientist had wrenched her snowmobile towards the cliff, skidding around in almost a complete circle before crashing.

"I think that something startled her," Connor guessed.

Kiki's heart raced at the sight of a mark pressed deep into the snow. A mark with a large central pad, five toes and five claw marks. She knew exactly what had startled Dr Mikkelsen – a polar bear!

Chapter Four
BEWARE – POLAR BEAR!

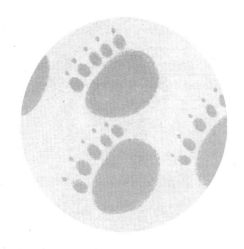

Kiki gasped. "Connor, look!"

Connor's face turned pale as he saw the giant paw print. "We have to be careful, Kiki," he said. His voice was quiet. "Polar bears look cute, but they are incredibly dangerous. They're stealthy hunters – fast, too. And their jaws are unbelievably powerful. Let's get back to the Beagle.

We might need to make a quick getaway."

"How will we see it?" Kiki said, glancing around. "It's white, and so's the snow . . ."

"A polar bear isn't actually white," said Connor.

Kiki stared. "What do you mean?"

Connor grinned at Kiki's expression. "Its strands of fur aren't white – they're transparent and hollow. That means the fur scatters the light, so it looks white."

"That must be good for camouflage," Kiki said.

Connor nodded. "And underneath their fur, their skin is black to absorb heat from the sun better. They're amazingly well adapted to life in the Arctic!" he said.

"Good to hear," Kiki said a little wryly as she scrambled on to the snowmobile as fast as she could.

"Just don't tell me how well adapted their teeth are next."

Connor climbed on behind Kiki. "After the crash, Dr Mikkelsen must have run away to hide," he guessed. "But nobody could outrun a full-size polar bear."

Kiki shivered. She hoped Dr Mikkelsen had a good hiding place. She pressed the "START" button. The Beagle roared to life.

"Where are we going to look?" Connor shouted over the sound of the engine.

Kiki studied Dr Mikkelsen's GPS tracker. The signal was strong and steady, some way off to the west of the crash site. She directed the Beagle away from the cliff, carefully skirting the polar bear prints.

Soon they were driving towards a broad plain of ice that seemed to stretch forever. Kiki had never seen anywhere so empty. She frowned at the coordinates on the Beagle's dashboard.

"The signal says Dr Mikkelsen should be nearby," she called to Connor behind her. "Can you see her?"

"There's nothing out here," Connor called back.

It was true. There was nothing in sight but the endless white horizon.

Kiki put on the brakes. "I think it's time we called the Exploration Station," she said.

The Beagle **BEEPED** in agreement. The sound echoed across the snow. Kiki pressed a button and a screen flickered into life on the Beagle's dashboard.

"Hey!" said Tamiko, from the familiar black-walled surroundings of the Exploration Station. "How's the mission going?"

Ollie appeared behind Tamiko. "Had a snowball fight yet?" he said.

"We've not had time for that, Ollie," said Kiki. "We urgently need to find a research scientist who's gone missing. Her name is Dr Mikkelsen. She had a snowmobile accident, but she didn't stay with the snowmobile and headed out here somewhere."

"And there's a polar bear," Connor added.

Leah appeared. "A polar bear?" she said eagerly. "Where?"

"That's the trouble," said Kiki. "We don't know. Can you help us? The GPS tracker is telling us Dr Mikkelsen is nearby, but we can't see anyone."

"We could search for thermal activity," Roshni suggested. "Astronomers use the technology to create thermal maps of planets like Jupiter."

"Great idea," said Leah. "Mammals like humans and polar bears are a lot warmer than the air and ground in the Arctic. If we use thermal imaging, we'll find Dr Mikkelsen in no time."

"Perfect," said Kiki. "Can you access the satellite data for our coordinates?"

The image on Kiki's screen changed from the faces of her friends to a dark screen dotted with spots of colour ranging from purple through to yellow. Two patches of thermal energy glowed before her eyes, standing in front of one much larger patch. Connor waved his arms around experimentally. One of the patches of energy on the screen did the same.

"Cool!" he said. "We're the little patches,

but what's making that big patch?" Connor looked behind them worriedly.

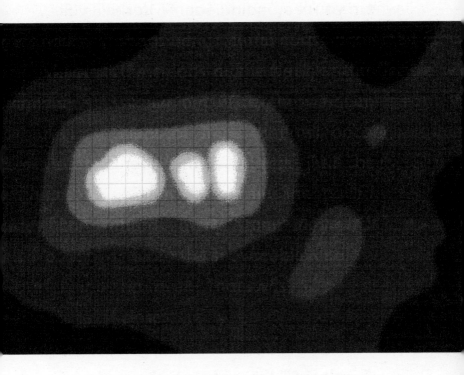

Kiki laughed. "That's the Beagle. The warm spot is its engine!"

"I'm just glad it's not the polar bear," Connor said.

"There's another patch of red thermal activity about twenty metres away from where you're standing," came Roshni's voice. "That must be your scientist friend. Head due west, and you'll find her."

"Got it," Kiki said. "Thanks team! Come on, Connor."

"Bye, Kiki!" chorused the other Explorers. "Bye, Connor! Good luck!"

Kiki and Connor left the Beagle and walked slowly west, as instructed.

"I don't understand where Dr Mikkelsen is," said Connor, gazing around as they walked. "There's no one—"

"Look out!" Kiki suddenly shouted.

Connor stopped. His eyes widened. His foot was just a few centimetres away from the edge of a crevasse! The crevasse was a huge split in the ice. Its sides were made of

bright blue ice, which seemed to glow as Kiki
looked at them. It was several metres deep,
and at the bottom the freezing water of the
Arctic sea churned dangerously.

"Dr Mikkelsen!" Kiki cried.

"Yes! Hi! I'm down here!" came a desperate voice from somewhere inside the crevasse. "Help me, please!"

Kiki got carefully on to her knees and peered over the edge. A woman with long dark hair, wearing thickly padded snow gear, stared up at her. She was standing on a ledge of ice that jutted out from the wall of the crevasse, around a metre above the black water.

"Don't worry," said Kiki. "We'll get you out of there!"

"Thank you," the woman said, shading her eyes against the glow of the blue ice. "I was running from the bear when the snow gave way beneath my feet and I ended up down here. I was lucky to land on this ledge. At least the bear couldn't chase me this far."

"Are you OK?" asked Connor, crouching beside Kiki.

The scientist nodded. "I'm not hurt, but I can't climb out. The walls of the crevasse are too steep."

"Quickly, Connor," Kiki said. "Let's see what equipment the Beagle has to help get her out of there!"

"Be careful!" Dr Mikkelsen called after them as they ran back to the Beagle. "The ice here is unstable. Not to mention the fact that the polar bear is still out there somewhere – and I think it's hungry!"

Chapter Five
SAVING THE SCIENTIST

Kiki rummaged frantically through the Beagle's storage compartments. It wasn't difficult to imagine the hungry polar bear breathing down her neck. The Beagle **BEEPED** and flashed its lights as she sifted through rations and bottles of water, until she found what she was looking for at the bottom: a harness and a set of strong ropes.

Connor helped her to fix one end of the ropes to the harness and the other to the Beagle. Then Kiki ran back to the crevasse, clutching the harness, the rope spilling out behind her.

"Remember the ice is unstable!" Connor called. He was still standing with the Beagle. "Stay well back, Kiki!"

Kiki knelt cautiously at the rim of the crevasse.

"I'm going to pass this harness down to you," she told the frightened scientist. "Can you fix it around yourself?"

Dr Mikkelsen nodded and reached upwards. Kiki lowered the harness down with the ropes until it was in Dr Mikkelsen's hands. As the scientist slid her arms inside, her fingers shook so much that she struggled to fix the buckle.

Kiki knew she had to keep Dr Mikkelsen calm. *Maybe I can distract her from how scary this is*, she thought. Her eye caught the deep blue colour of the ice ledge where the scientist was standing.

"What makes the ice down there so blue, Dr Mikkelsen?" she asked.

"This is old ice," Dr Mikkelsen said, as she fought to buckle the harness. "It was once under a lot of pressure. The pressure forced out all the air bubbles, changing its density and colour." Her fingers stopped shaking as she looked around at the blue glow. "This ice was once part of a great glacier," she said. "Most of the top layer has melted away, leaving only this."

There was a sudden click. Dr Mikkelsen grinned up at Kiki – she was clearly relieved that the harness was now securely buckled.

Kiki felt a rush of relief too. She turned to signal to Connor.

Connor revved the Beagle's engine, sending up a spray of ice. The Beagle flashed its lights.

"Ready to get out of there, Dr Mikkelsen?" Connor called.

The Beagle flashed its light again and beeped urgently. *Beep beep BEEP!*

Kiki held up her hand. "Wait, Connor!" she said. "The Beagle's trying to warn you."

Connor looked down at the dashboard.

"What? Why?"

"You don't need to drive at full power," Kiki explained. "Snowmobiles have got spiked treads, so the wheels won't lose grip like a car's do in snow – the Beagle will go really fast, and Dr Mikkelsen will come flying out of the crevasse like a cork popping from a bottle!"

"Got it!" called Connor. He gently drove the Beagle away from the crevasse. The spiked treads gripped the ice firmly and the rope grew taut.

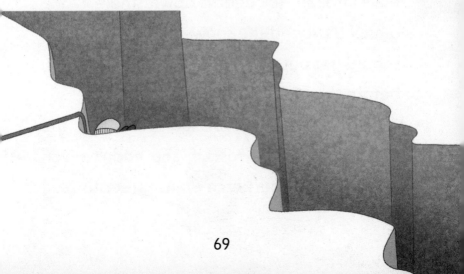

"That's it," Kiki called into the crevasse, as Dr Mikkelsen started to rise up, suspended by her harness. "Steady . . . You're nearly out . . . There you go . . . Got you!"

Kiki seized Dr Mikkelsen's hands and helped her scramble over the edge. She sprawled weakly at Kiki's feet, breathing heavily. Connor jumped off the Beagle and joined them, helping Kiki to unbuckle the harness and stow the rope away.

"Thank you," said the scientist, getting to her feet. "If it hadn't been for you, I would have frozen to death down there." She glanced around the snowy plain. "I think we should get out of here. As quickly as we can, before the bear comes back."

Kiki felt a thrill of fear. With all the excitement of the rescue, she hadn't given a thought to the fierce white predator still lurking about, looking for a meal.

They all climbed on to the Beagle. It was a little snug with three of them, but Beagle **BEEPED** happily.

"Should we take you to the research centre?" asked Kiki, as the Beagle picked up speed.

"Yes, please," Dr Mikkelsen replied. "We still need help to free our research vessel from the ice."

"Then let's go!" said Kiki.

She steered the Beagle back the way they'd come, following the snowy tracks they'd made. They carefully skirted Dr Mikkelsen's ruined snowmobile and headed on across a wide ice plain. Following the coordinates Dr Andersen had given them, they passed craggy outcroppings and snow whipped into fantastical shapes. After half an hour, the buildings of the Arctic research centre came into view on the horizon. Not far beyond the buildings, Kiki glimpsed the grey line of the sea. A huge ship lay at anchor. Its bow was a strange, bulging shape.

"That's an ice breaker!" Kiki said. "They can use it to free the research ship."

"It's just what we need," Dr Mikkelsen agreed.

Kiki parked the Beagle in a wide sweep of ice outside the research centre's main building. They were just climbing off the snowmobile's padded seat when an eerie sound wailed across the ice. It rose and fell, urgent and insistent.

"That's the alarm," said Dr Mikkelsen. "I wonder what's happened?"

Kiki pulled her coat a little closer against the wind. She caught a flash of movement out of the corner of her eye.

Something large and white was padding towards them. It placed its huge paws carefully on the ice, as if it was testing the ground. Its nose was raised, a dot of black against the white snow.

The polar bear was here – and it was looking right at them!

Chapter Six
MOTHER BEAR

Kiki stared at the polar bear. Her feet felt as if they were stuck to the spot. It was pretty amazing, staring into the eyes of such an incredible predator.

Connor grabbed her arm. "Come on!" he said. "We have to get inside!"

Dr Mikkelsen was already running across the wide space in front of the building. She turned and shouted for them to follow. The polar bear was still watching Kiki and Connor.

"Quickly!" Connor shouted.

Kiki ran. The nearest door seemed so far away but Dr Mikkelsen made it inside and held it open for them. At any moment, Kiki imagined the weight of the bear crashing into them, and knocking them down into the snow. Gasping, she ran as fast as she could. She and Connor burst through the set of double doors.

The heat inside the building hit Kiki with a rush. Dr Mikkelsen slammed the doors shut behind them.

A man with a grey beard and heavy glasses hurried up to them. "My name is Dr Bridgers," he said. "Are you okay?"

Kiki, Connor and Dr Mikkelsen looked at each other, then nodded.

"That was crazy," gasped Kiki, holding

her sides and breathing heavily.

Connor looked a little green. "I really thought the bear was going to catch us!" he said.

Kiki realised they were in a large room with windows all along one side. Several other people were there, gathered around the windows and watching the polar bear outside.

The bear was padding past the main building. Kiki and Connor hurried to the window to watch. Kiki felt a thrill run down her spine as she watched the bear's enormous paws moving soundlessly through the snow, swaying and sniffing the air. Kiki could hardly believe how close she was to such a beautiful, dangerous animal.

Connor suddenly gasped and clutched Kiki's arm. "She's not by herself," he said. "Look, she's got cubs!"

"Oh my GOSH," Kiki whispered.

At first, the two little shapes following the polar bear were difficult to see. Their fur was whiter than their mother's. They blended perfectly with the snow as they rolled and played together, biting each other's fluffy snowball-like ears.

"They fight like my little brothers," Kiki said with a giggle.

They watched, holding their breath, as the mother bear strode on past the windows. She was leading the cubs towards a stretch of ice not far from the research centre. Kiki could see a glimmer of stone-grey water shining through a hole in the ice. The mother bear stopped, and glanced at her cubs. "Come along," she seemed to be saying. "I have something important to show you."

"It's another seal hole," said Connor. He pressed his face closer to the glass, shielding his eyes to cut out the glare. "Like the one where we saw the ringed seals. She's teaching them to hunt. They'll wait until a seal comes up for air and then try to catch it." He gave a sigh of happiness. "I can't believe I'm seeing this. I feel so lucky."

"It's a wonderful sight for us," said Dr Bridgers. He gazed out of the window at the little family. "But I've spent my life studying polar bears, and they never used to come this close to human activity. The ice is melting, you see, and their habitat is shrinking. They have no choice but to travel further south than they usually would to search for food."

"You study polar bears?" asked Connor eagerly. "That's awesome!"

Dr Bridgers laughed. "Come," he said. "You might enjoy this." He led Kiki and Connor across the room, towards a long white table covered in specimen jars and notebooks. He selected something long and white, with a sharp point at one end. "A polar bear tooth," he said, passing it to Kiki. "We find them in the field sometimes."

Kiki's mouth fell open as she stared at the huge fang she was holding. It was as long as her hand!

"You can see why polar bears are such successful hunters," said Dr Bridgers. "But these days, life is hard for them. If the Earth continues to warm up, they will lose their hunting grounds all together."

"That's terrible," said Kiki.

Back at the window, the polar bear had given up on the ice hole and was padding away now, followed by her two fluffy cubs. Soon they had vanished, leaving only a trail of pawprints behind them.

"That was amazing," Connor said. Kiki had to agree.

"What brings you out here?" asked Dr Bridgers. "We don't usually have visitors dropping into the research centre."

Dr Mikkelsen joined them. "These two came to find me. I'm from *The Explorer*. It's trapped in the ice." And she quickly told him everything that had happened.

"Can you help, Dr Bridgers?" Kiki asked.

"I'll alert the crew of the ice breaker," said Dr Bridgers at once. "And we'll send someone out to fetch the damaged snowmobile. We can repair it here. Can you return to *The Explorer* and let the crew know that help is on its way? We'll bring the ice breaker over as soon as we can."

"We're on it," said Kiki at once. "Let's go, Connor!"

Chapter Seven

KIKI'S RESCUE PLAN

The cold air wrapped itself around Kiki again as she, Connor, and Dr Mikkelsen left the research centre and headed for the Beagle. She fixed on her helmet and snuggled deeper into her snowgear. *The snow smelled amazing,* she thought – as cool and clean as a long drink on a hot day.

The Beagle **BEEPED** a greeting and gave

a sort of purr as they climbed on.

"Talkative snowmobile you have here," said Dr Mikkelsen, patting the seat.

"The Beagle always has plenty to say," Kiki said with a laugh. She programmed the coordinates for *The Explorer*. The Beagle's dashboard lit up eagerly, like a dog excited for a walk. Kiki revved the engine. They pulled away from the research centre and drove off across the snow, doubling back the way they had come.

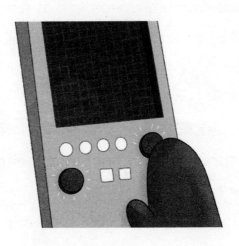

Gulls screamed and wheeled in the heavy grey sky as they rode back across the ice plains. Snow spattered Kiki's goggles. The Beagle ploughed steadily through the landscape. The white horizon stretched away almost as far as Kiki could see. With no landmarks to help them find their way, Kiki was glad they had both the coordinates for *The Explorer* and their own tracks from earlier to follow.

"There it is!" shouted Connor, pointing out the red hull on the horizon. The broken ice shelf had nudged the ship even further off-centre. Kiki didn't remember it tilting quite so badly.

"Oh no!" said Connor. "Why's it tipping over like that?"

Dr Mikkelsen shaded her eyes. "The ice is crowding it and pushing it to one side. The sooner the ice breaker can get here, the better."

They zoomed towards *The Explorer*. Soon Kiki was once more approaching the icy slope where they had first parked the Beagle and boarded the ship. She followed her own tracks back up. The caterpillar tread gripped the snow as she turned off the engine and took off her helmet.

Dr Andersen must have heard the approaching engine. He was already on the deck to meet them, looking anxious. His face cleared when he saw Dr Mikkelsen with Connor and Kiki.

"Thank goodness you're all safe!" he said as he helped the scientist and the Secret Explorers aboard. "What happened? Is help coming?"

"A polar bear chased me and I fell into a crevasse," said Dr Mikkelsen. She shot Kiki and Connor a grateful glance. "But these two rescued me."

Kiki and Connor filled in the rest of the details for Dr Andersen: the snowmobile crash, the research centre, and the bear with her two cubs. Kiki staggered a little as she spoke. It was hard to stay upright on the listing deck.

"I'm glad the ice breaker is on its way," Dr Andersen said. "Come with me to the bridge. We'll make an announcement to the crew."

They followed Dr Andersen through the ship's door and up the metal steps to the bridge. At the top, Kiki clung to the edge of the ship's control panel. The way *The Explorer* sloped beneath her feet made her feel off-balance.

When Dr Andersen announced over the ship's speaker system that help was coming, Kiki heard a faint cheer from the crew down below.

They all gasped as the ship tilted even further.

"This isn't good," said Kiki. "When the ice breaker does its work, *The Explorer* is going to move around even more. We need to get it upright, or..."

"... Or it might tip over completely," finished Connor. He gulped.

"You're right, Kiki," said Dr Andersen. "But how can we get *The Explorer* upright again?"

Kiki thought hard. "Imagine that the ship is a seesaw," she said. She demonstrated with her arm, tilting it up and down. "If one person sits on the end of a seesaw, it goes down. But if someone else sits on the other end too, it balances out."

Connor's face cleared. "I think I get it!"

"The ship is tilting to starboard," said Kiki. "We need to move as much cargo and equipment to the port side as we can. The extra weight should make it tilt upright."

Connor scratched his head. "Which way's starboard again?"

"Starboard is right; port is left," said Kiki. 'Port' has four letters, and so does 'left'. That's how I remember it."

"Excellent plan, Kiki!" said Dr Andersen. He switched on the speaker system again. "Attention crew," he said. "Move cargo to port side. I repeat, move cargo to port side. Over."

Moments later, *The Explorer* was bustling as the crew hauled boxes, crates, weather-reading equipment, cans of food, bags of flour and sugar, ice drills, coils of metal chains, and data recorders from one side of the ship to the other. Kiki and Connor pitched in, carrying whatever they could lift.

"Ice breaker ahead!" someone shouted.

Kiki and Connor ran up the metal steps to the bridge, clinging to each other to stay upright. Through the ice-splattered windows, they saw the hulking ship with the strange hull they had last seen anchored near the research centre. The ship was churning through the sea towards them, effortlessly throwing up chunks of ice and sprays of water. The metal floor began to rock under their feet as the wash from the ice breaker struck the research vessel's hull.

"It's massive," said Connor with awe. "How does it break through? Isn't the ice several metres deep?"

"It works through the weight of its hull and the design of its bow," Kiki explained as they watched the approaching ship. "It looks like it's just smashing through the ice, but it's actually crushing it from above. The ship presses down on it and breaks it up."

The movement of the approaching ice breaker was making *The Explorer* rock more violently now. Dislodged ice crashed and clattered against the hull. With a horrible creak, *The Explorer* lurched even further sideways. Connor grabbed on to a nearby table, which was fixed to the floor of the bridge.

"The cargo we moved isn't enough," Kiki guessed. "We need more weight on the port side."

Dr Andersen hurried back to the speaker system. "More cargo to port side! Quickly!"

Kiki looked around in dismay. Despite all their efforts, the ship was tilting even further to the left. If they couldn't get it upright again, they would capsize and sink before the ice breaker even reached them!

But the Secret Explorers never gave up.

Kiki and Connor took the stairs two at a time. Crew members ran about, trying to move more cargo to the port side of the ship. *The Explorer* groaned and shuddered. "We can't let the ship capsize!" she said. "No one could survive for long in the freezing Arctic water..."

She had an idea. How many crew worked on a ship this size?

"All crew to port side!" Kiki shouted, waving her arms to get everyone's attention. "Everyone, move!"

Everyone rushed to the port side of the ship, Kiki and Connor leading the way. Kiki felt the ship tilt very slightly upright again.

"It's not enough," said Connor. Fear flashed across his face.

"We've moved everything we can," Dr Andersen said, breathing hard from the

effort. "There's nothing more we can do."

Kiki glanced swiftly out of the porthole beside her. The ice breaker was almost here. Would there be a ship left for it to rescue?

"Stay here," she said. "I've got one more idea..."

"Where are you going, Kiki?" Connor called as Kiki darted through a door.

"No time to explain," Kiki called back. "Just stay port side!"

The deck was slippery with ice and seawater. The air juddered with groaning ice and the propellers of the fast-approaching ice breaker. Kiki ran as quickly as she could across the deck and leaped ashore, onto the icy slope where she had left the Beagle. She sprang on to the snowmobile's padded seat and gunned the engine.

"Come on, Beagle," she said. "We'll make the jump together!"

The Beagle flashed in agreement. Kiki revved the throttle and released the brake. With a roar, the snowmobile soared off the icy slope – and landed hard on the port side of the deck.

Everything shook with the impact. Slowly but surely, *The Explorer* began to shift upright!

The ice breaker smashed through the

last section of the frozen sea surrounding *The Explorer*. With a great groan and a shudder, the ship tilted fully upright, smashing through the pack ice – and settled, at last, to float free on the open water.

They'd done it!

Chapter Eight
MISSION ACCOMPLISHED

Kiki and Connor sat on the bridge, watching the crew of *The Explorer* out in the bright, cold Arctic air. They were putting all their research equipment back into the correct positions, and moving crates and winches around the deck. The ship had drawn up to a concrete dockside, and on the shore, delivery trucks were bringing fresh supplies.

Soon, Dr Andersen and his team would sail deep into the Arctic Circle to complete their important research. It was vital that they stocked up on all the food and drink they would need. It would be several months before they returned to shore.

Dr Mikkelsen was standing at the controls of the ship with Dr Andersen.

"Do you want to lower the ramp, Kiki?" offered Dr Mikkelsen.

Kiki's eyes lit up. "Would I?!" she said enthusiastically. "Yes, please!" Scrambling out of her chair, she hurried across to the panel of dials and switches and screens. She ran her fingers over the controls. *This is an engineer's dream come true!* she thought. There's a gyro compass, a radar, an echo sounder, a speed and log device . . .

"It's that one!" said Dr Andersen with a laugh, pointing out a large black switch.

Kiki flipped the switch. At once she heard the grinding sound of the ramp, lowering itself to the dock. Their mission was over, and it was time to say goodbye.

Kiki reluctantly left the huge navigation panel and followed Connor and the two scientists out of the bridge and down the echoing metal stairs to the deck. Dr Bridgers was there, too – he had travelled on the ice breaker.

Kiki reached into her pocket. "This is yours, Dr Bridgers," she said, drawing out the polar bear tooth. "I forgot to give it back to you."

"Keep it," Dr Bridgers said with a smile, "as a thank you for all you have done."

"Thank you," said Kiki and Connor. They shook the three scientists' hands.

"I hope you make some cool discoveries on your research trip!" said Connor.

"So do I," said Dr Mikkelsen warmly. "If you hadn't come along . . . Well, I wouldn't be going on any more research trips. I'd still be stuck down that crevasse!"

The Beagle was waiting for them on the deck. It flashed its lights as Kiki and Connor took their places on its padded seat. Kiki started up the engine and drove the Beagle down the ramp and on to the concrete dockside.

"Oh!" she gasped. Something cold was sliding down the back of her jacket.

"We couldn't leave without ONE little snowball fight!" Connor said with a grin. He brushed snow off his gloves.

Kiki grinned back and scooped up a snowball of her own. "Gotcha!" she cried, as she launched it on top of Connor's head.

Laughing, they sped along the white coastline. The snowy landscape grew brighter and brighter. Kiki squinted as the Beagle accelerated with enormous speed. Then, with a blinding flash, Kiki and Connor were back at the Exploration Station.

The other Secret Explorers gathered around them, talking and laughing.

"Welcome back!" exclaimed Roshni. "You've got snow in your hair, Connor."

"Not as much snow as I've got down my back!" said Kiki with a laugh. She climbed off the Beagle. "Oh wow, it feels so warm in here!"

"Crazy trip, huh?" said Ollie enthusiastically. "We watched the whole thing on the computers!"

"It was the best," said Connor.

With a grin, Kiki dived into her pocket

and pulled out the enormous polar bear tooth once more. Tamiko whistled. "If I didn't know better, I'd say that was from a dinosaur!" she said.

Kiki proudly placed the tooth inside one of the display cabinets that lined the walls of the Exploration Station. Everyone clapped and whistled, patting Connor and Kiki on the backs. Another successful mission was complete.

The door at the back of the room was glowing. It was time to go home.

"Bye, Connor," said Kiki. "That was fun, wasn't it?"

Connor nodded. "Really fun. See you next time!"

After waving to everyone else, Kiki walked towards the bright light. As she closed her eyes, she felt the familiar blast of air rushing across her skin. The dazzle faded gradually as she opened her eyes, blinking in the warm dusty air of home. She was back on the steps outside her school.

Kiki walked dreamily down them. *I wonder how the ship is getting on?* she thought, picturing it sailing through the icy sea. She unlocked her bike and swung her leg over the seat. The Beagle was a little more comfortable than her bicycle, and driving the snowmobile had been fun. But she was glad to be home, in the familiar sunshine, with her bag of tools hanging at her side. The memory of the cold, wet snowball down her neck faded as she cycled home, humming to herself in the warm afternoon air.

KIKI'S
MISSION NOTES

THE ARCTIC ✳✳

The Arctic is a huge frozen wilderness at the top of the Earth. It's one of the coldest and most extreme habitats on Earth. Most of the Arctic is made up of the frozen Arctic Ocean, but there is also land around the outer edges known as tundra.

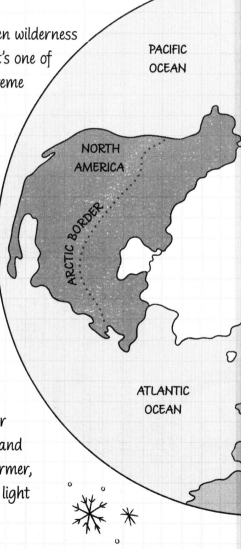

PACIFIC
OCEAN

NORTH
AMERICA

ARCTIC BORDER

ATLANTIC
OCEAN

SEASONS

There are two seasons in the Arctic. During the freezing winter it is dark almost all day and night. The Summer is warmer, but still cold, but it stays light most or all of the time.

THE NORTH POLE

At the centre of the Arctic is the North Pole – the northern most point on Earth. At the North Pole, the ice never melts, but further south the ice in the Arctic melts during the summer.

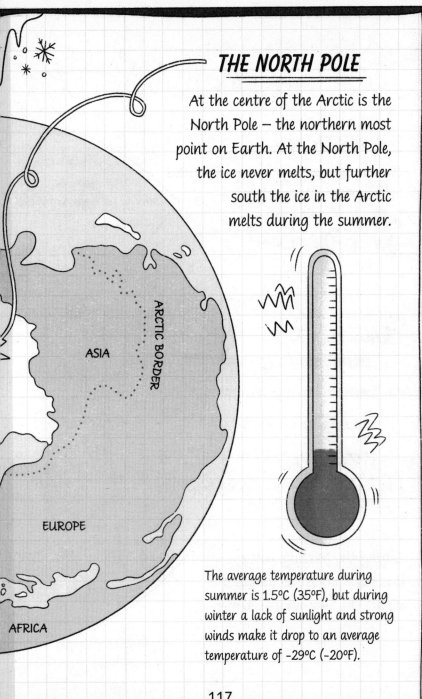

ASIA

ARCTIC BORDER

EUROPE

AFRICA

The average temperature during summer is 1.5°C (35°F), but during winter a lack of sunlight and strong winds make it drop to an average temperature of -29°C (-20°F).

POLAR BEARS

THE POLAR BEAR IS THE WORLD'S LARGEST LAND CARNIVORE!

Eyes: Polar bears have an extra clear eyelid that helps them to see underwater and in snowstorms.

FACT FILE

Latin name: Ursus maritimus

Animal type: Mammal

Location: The Arctic

Length: Up to 2.5m (8¼ft) long

Weight: Up to 1,000kg (2,200lb)

Polar bears can run at 40kph (25mph) and swim at 10kph (6mph). They can swim for 100km (60 miles) without having to take a rest!

Claws: Sharp claws help polar bears grip the ice.

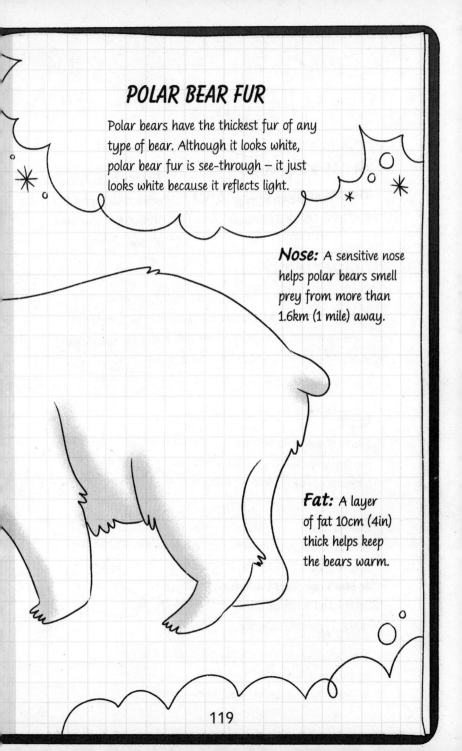

POLAR BEAR FUR

Polar bears have the thickest fur of any type of bear. Although it looks white, polar bear fur is see-through – it just looks white because it reflects light.

Nose: A sensitive nose helps polar bears smell prey from more than 1.6km (1 mile) away.

Fat: A layer of fat 10cm (4in) thick helps keep the bears warm.

119

LIFE ON THE ICE

Despite the freezing cold, people have lived in the Arctic for thousands of years. Because it's too cold to grow crops, people in the Arctic developed special hunting, fishing, and crafting techniques to survive.

ARCTIC PEOPLES

About 4 million people live in the Arctic. Most live in modern cities and towns near the coastline, but some live in remote communities and still follow the traditions of their ancestors. Here are just a few:

* ### Inuit
  The Inuit people are native to Greenland, Canada, and Alaska. For thousands of years, they have relied on hunting and gathering. Today, many live together in small communities.

* ### Sami
  The Sami people of northern Scandinavia and Russia have herded reindeer in the Arctic wilderness for centuries. Today, most Sami live in towns on the Arctic Tundra.

* ### Dolgan
  The Dolgan people of northern Russia live in some of the coldest conditions on Earth. They rely on reindeer for transport, food, and clothing.

IGLOOS

Ancient Inuits lived in houses made of bone, wood, stone, and animal fur. But on long hunting trips they built temporary shelters called igloos using blocks of snow. Today, Inuits live in modern homes, but they still build igloos on long hunting trips.

Thick walls made of snow keep out the cold and trap heat inside from escaping — making igloos surprisingly warm!

ARCTIC TOOLS

While the traditional skills and tools of their ancestors are very important to Arctic peoples, many of them now combine them with more modern ways of life. New inventions, such as the snowmobile have made life in the Arctic much easier.

SNOWSHOES

SNOWMOBILE

KAYAKS

SLEDGE

QUIZ

1   What is the name of a ship's control centre?

2   What type of seals do Kiki and Connor encounter?

3   True or false: The left side of a ship is called the port side.

4   What technology helps the team find Dr Mikkelsen?

5   What vehicle does the Beagle turn into that helps the Secret Explorers travel across the ice?

6   What ships are used to destroy large areas of ice?

7   True or false: Ice cores allow scientists to study what Earth was like in the past.

SEARCH FOR GULLS!

There are 4 herring gulls to spot in this book. Can you find them all?

They look like this!

Check your answers on page 127

GLOSSARY

ASTRONOMER
A scientist who studies space

BRIDGE
The command centre of a ship

CAMOUFLAGE
Colours or patterns on an animal's skin, fur, or feathers that help it blend into the environment

CAPSIZE
When a ship is overturned in water

CARGO
Objects carried on a ship

CLIMATE CHANGE
Change in temperature and weather across the Earth that can be natural or caused by human activity

CREVASSE
A deep crack in
the ice

CREW
A group of people
who work on a ship

GLACIER
Large mass of ice
that moves slowly
down a slope

GPS
A radio navigation
system that enables
people to determine
exact locations and
get directions

HORIZON
The point where the
land meets the sky

HULL
The main part
of a ship

ICE BREAKER
A ship used to break
up large areas of ice

LABORATORY
A location where
science experiments
take place

PLATEAU
A large area of high, flat land

PORT
The left side of a ship

PORTHOLE
A small round window on a ship

PREDATOR
An animal that hunts and eats other animals

SNOWMOBILE
A vehicle used to travel over the snow and ice

SPECIMEN JARS
Containers used to hold objects for scientific study

STARBOARD
The right side of a ship

VESSEL
A boat or ship

Quiz answers

1. The bridge

2. Ringed seals

3. True

4. Thermal imaging

5. Snowmobile

6. Icebreakers

7. True

For Oscar

Text for DK by Working Partners Ltd
9 Kingsway, London WC2B 6XF
With special thanks to Lucy Courtenay

Design by Collaborate Ltd
Illustrator Ellie O'Shea
Consultant Derek Harvey

Acquisitions Editor James Mitchem
Designer Sonny Flynn
Publishing Coordinator Issy Walsh
Senior Production Editor Robert Dunn
Production Controller John Casey
Publishing Director Sarah Larter

First published in Great Britain in 2021 by
Dorling Kindersley Limited
One Embassy Gardens, 8 Viaduct Gardens,
London, SW11 7AY

A CIP catalogue record for this book
is available from the British Library.
ISBN: 978-0-2414-4229-6

Printed and bound in Great Britain by
Clays Ltd, Elcograf S.p.A.

For the curious
www.dk.com

The publisher would like to thank Caroline Twomey for proofreading,
and Lynne Murray for picture library assistance.